THE MUFFIN MUNCHER

Written by:
STEPHEN COSGROVE
Illustrated by:
ROBIN JAMES

Printed in U.S.A.

ISBN #0-915396-02-5 THE MUFFIN MUNCHER

P.O. Box 9123 Queen Anne Station
Seattle, Washington 98109

Dedicated to Phil, Norm, Gary, Byron, Eva, Edris, and most of all, Joanne and Jennifer. Without them this book could not have been written.

Many, many years ago in the far corner of a very poor country stood the poorest of poor castles.

Not only did the villagers of the castle lack riches and valuables, but they were poor in spirit—for they had done nothing to be proud of.

The only way they had survived at all was by baking and selling the most delicious and delectable muffins in the land.

Every morning the King, who was also the head baker, would bake up a fresh batch of muffins. When he had finished and the muffins were baked and still warm from the ovens, the villagers would load their carts and set off for the other villages in the kingdom.

There was never any problem in selling the muffins since they were the finest ever baked. But because the villagers were so poor, they had to use all the money they had earned to buy more firewood and flour in order to make more muffins.

So, day in and day out, the head baker, who was also the king, would build up the giant fires in the ovens and bake muffins and muffins and muffins.

He would slowly mix all the ingredients in a big cracked bowl, pour the batter into the muffin tins, and carefully put them in the ovens to bake.

The villagers were just barely surviving. As if things weren't bad enough for them, there appeared at the castle one day a great and monstrous dragon. Now, this was not your everyday, run-of-the-mill dragon dragon. He was a rather enormous, slightly overweight, muffin munching dragon.

With crumbs still on his face from the muffins he'd eaten at the last castle he'd visited, the dragon came trotting down the hill, right up to the drawbridge.

Taking one look at the dragon, the villagers hastily ran over the drawbridge and hustled into the castle to hide.

The dragon took a great long sniff. "Ahh," he mumbled, "I smell muffins!" This castle, he decided, smelled like a nice place to stay. He picked up his suitcase and moved in, right under the drawbridge.

He was very tired from his long journey, so he unpacked his pillow, his pajamas and the picture of his pony, curled up and fell fast asleep.

The next morning the villagers looked out of their castle windows and thought that the dragon was gone. Breathing a sigh of relief, they calmly began preparing for another day.

After loading their wagons with fresh warm muffins, they set off across the draw-bridge, over the soundly sleeping dragon. With all the rattling from the wagons, the dragon awoke with a shudder.

He yawned once, stretched twice, and peeked over the edge to se what was going on. "So that's it, huh? Those muffins look so good and I am very hungry!"

He thought and thought, and finally came up with a plan.

He jumped up on the drawbridge right in front of the villagers, tried to look very ferocious, and roared loudly: "Stop, or I shall burn up your drawbridge!" Then, to be just a little more convincing, he blew a little flame and puffed three smoke rings.

"Henceforth," he rumbled, "you shall each give me ten of your most delicious muffins as your toll to cross my bridge."

"But this is our drawbridge!" they cried.

"Well, if I burn it up, it won't be anybody's drawbridge," said the dragon.

The villagers thought and talked for a moment and finally agreed to give the dragon his muffins. They barely had enough money to buy firewood, let alone enough wood to build a new drawbridge.

From then on, every wagon that crossed the drawbridge left the dragon ten absolutely delicious muffins. With crumbs all around him, the dragon would sit there, contentedly stuffing those scrumptious muffins away.

This probably would have gone on to this very day except for one slight problem. The dragon was eating so many muffins that the villagers did not have enough to sell. Because of that, they didn't have enough money to buy firewood for the ovens, or even flour to bake more muffins.

They would return every day with fewer and fewer supplies, until one day they all came home with nothing.

The next morning the head baker, who was also the king, could not fire up the great ovens because there was no firewood. He could not use his big cracked bowl, because he had no flour or supplies to put in it to make muffins.

With a heavy heart and a tear in his eye, the baker sat sadly on a pile of empty flour sacks and cried, "We have no more supplies to make muffins, and no more wood to light the fires. We cannot bake any more muffins, and the dragon will burn our drawbridge down. What are we ever to do?

That very same day the dragon woke up, brushed his teeth, combed his hair, and prepared for another day of muffin munching.

He waited and waited and waited. No wagons came, no muffins came, and the dragon's stomach began to rumble, grumble and growl. He tried eating a few of the crumbs that had dropped on the ground the day before, but that didn't satisfy his hunger; besides, they were stale. "No muffins!" he grumbled as his stomach rumbled and growled. "No muffins!"

Finally he decided to enter the castle and find out what had happened to all his muffins.

The dragon wandered through the castle until he reached the bakery. Then he peeked inside. "Where are my muffins?" he rumbled. "I've been waiting and waiting and waiting! Where are my muffins?"

The head baker, who was also the king, walked up to the dragon as bravely as he could. "Mr. Dragon," he said, "we are poor villagers, living in a poor castle which has very little. Before you came, the muffins we sold barely paid for our firewood and supplies. Now that we have to give you so many muffins, we can't afford to buy enough firewood, and our ovens have no heat."

That poor dragon was so very confused. He wanted some muffins because he was so hungry. But at the same time he felt sorry for the baker and the other villagers who lived in the castle.

The dragon thought and thought. Finally, a great big smile crossed his face. "I have it!" he shouted. He asked the head baker, who was also the king, to call all the villagers to a castle conference so that he could tell them of his marvelous plan.

The villagers happily began to cheer and shout as he finished, for surely the dragon had solved the castle's problems, and his own, forevermore.

Then and for always, the dragon heated the ovens of the bakery with his mighty flame. With the extra money they saved by not having to buy firewood, the villagers could easily afford to leave a generous stack of muffins within easy reach of the muffin-munching dragon.

WHILE HEATING UP THE OVENS
WITH A LOT OF STYLE AND GRACE,
THE MUFFIN MUNCHER SMILES A SMILE
WITH CRUMBS UPON HIS FACE.

Left: Stephen Cosgrove   Right: Robin James